James Mayhew
presents

Ella Bella
❋ BALLERINA ❋
~ *and* ~

A Midsummer Night's Dream

For Raffi Bowen
~fairy ballerina and shooting star!
J. M.

First edition for North America published in 2015
by Barron's Educational Series, Inc.

Text and illustrations © James Mayhew 2015

First published in 2015 by Orchard Books
338 Euston Road, London, NW1 3BH
Orchard Books Australia
Level 17/207 Kent Street, Sydney, NSW 2000

Orchard Books is an imprint of
Hachette Children's Group and published by
The Watts Publishing Group Limited,
a Hachette UK company.
www.hachette.co.uk

All inquiries should be addressed to:
Barron's Educational Series, Inc.
250 Wireless Boulevard
Hauppauge, New York 11788
www.barronseduc.com

ISBN: 978-0-7641-6797-3

Library of Congress Catalog Card No.: 2015933546

Date of Manufacture: July 2015
Manufactured by: RR Donnelley Asia
Printing Solutions Limited, Dongguan, China

Printed in China
9 8 7 6 5 4 3 2 1

James Mayhew
presents

Ella Bella
BALLERINA
~ *and* ~

A Midsummer Night's Dream

Ella Bella and her friends were at the old
theater, getting ready for their ballet class.
"Today, my darlings, you can try on some
costumes," said their teacher, Madame Rosa.

Everyone tried on something different.
Ella Bella chose a fairy costume with little
purple flowers.
"You all look wonderful," said Madame Rosa.
"Now we need some music!"

Madame Rosa opened her magical music box
and out poured a shimmering tune.
"This is *A Midsummer Night's Dream*
by Felix Mendelssohn," she said.
"It's based on Shakespeare's story
about fairies and elves. There is
even a fairy king and queen!"

"It does sound just like fairy music,"
said Ella Bella, dreamily.
"Let's all dance like fairies and elves!"
said Madame Rosa.

The children danced to the music,
waving their arms and twirling around.
"Enchanting, my dears," said Madame Rosa.

All too soon the lesson was over, and the children went to get changed . . . except Ella Bella.

She wanted to have one more dance in her fairy flower costume, as it was so beautiful.

Ella Bella opened the lid of
the music box. As the fairy tune played,
she began to dance.

"Pssst!" someone called.
Ella Bella saw an elf smiling at her.
"May I borrow those flowers in your hair?
I have searched the world over for them."

"My name is Puck," said the elf. "Oberon,
King of Fairyland, needs those flowers to
win back the heart of Titania, his fairy queen.
It seems she no longer loves him . . . instead,
she spends all her days playing with fairies
and elves."

"What will the flowers do?" asked Ella Bella. "They are magic flowers, and they will help with some midsummer mischief!" said Puck. "Now, take my hand, fairy child! Oberon awaits!"

Ella Bella realized they were flying high above a forest. It was a warm summer night and the sky shimmered with stars. The moon covered the trees in a silvery light, as fairies flitted around like fireflies and moths.

Ella Bella and Puck landed beside
a great, old oak tree where Oberon,
King of Fairyland, was waiting.

"I found the magic flowers," said Puck.
"Well done," said Oberon. "They are called
Love in Idleness. I will use them to cast a
midsummer spell on Queen Titania."

"How will the spell work?" asked Ella Bella,
with a curtsy.
"Titania will fall in love with the first creature
she sees," laughed Oberon. "I hope it will be
a very silly kind of beast! Perhaps then she
will remember that I am her true love."

"Come on," said Puck. "Let's find someone really funny for the fairy queen to fall in love with!"

They giggled and tiptoed off between the trees.

In a clearing, some friends were practicing a play.

A man named Bottom was reading the
script, but he kept getting the words wrong.
"Oh dear," he said. "I must practice more,
or I shall make a fool of myself!"

"Let's play a trick on Bottom," said Puck. "He reminds me of a silly donkey!"

Puck sprinkled some magic on Bottom, and he began to change . . .

He grew longs ears and a furry snout!

Bottom had no idea he looked so funny
and wondered why his friends all ran away!
He set off into the woods after them.

"Now he is the perfect love for our
queen!" giggled Puck.

Bottom found a grove filled with flowers. There slept the beautiful fairy queen, Titania. She was surrounded by fairies singing.

Oberon had already put the magic
flower juice upon Titania's eyes.
Then, Bottom tried singing, too . . .

Titania awoke to Bottom's braying. "Oh, my lovely!" she said, as she stroked Bottom's ears and gazed into his eyes. It was quite clear that Titania was in love with him!

They danced under the moon, and then, at last, fell asleep in each other's arms.

"They look so silly!" giggled Ella Bella and Puck. Oberon appeared. "Yes, and when Titania awakes she will hope this donkey was only a midsummer dream," he smiled. "Now, remove the spell from the foolish Bottom."

Puck waved his hands, and Bottom's donkey ears vanished, and his own face was restored. He ran off to find his friends.

Already the moon was fading and the sky
was growing pale. When Titania awoke,
she saw Oberon and smiled.

"Oh, my dearest king, I am so glad to see
you," she said. "I dreamed I was in love
with a donkey!"
"My queen," said Oberon. "Will you stay
with me always?"
"Always, my love," said Titania.

Midsummer Night was over and everything was back as it should be. "And now, farewell, fairy Ella Bella!" said Puck. "And thank you!" Ella Bella waved as he flew off into the sky like a shooting star!

The music stopped and Ella Bella saw she
was back in the old theater. There on the
floor were the magic flowers. She carefully
picked them up.

Madame Rosa came to see how she was doing.
"Here you are," said Ella Bella, handing her
the flowers.

"Thank you," said Madame Rosa. "Now, hurry out
of your costume. Your mother is waiting and it will
soon be dark, and that's fairy time!"

On the way home with her mother,
Ella Bella looked up at the sky
and saw the moon.

Suddenly, a shooting star flew across the sky.
She smiled as she thought of the fairy king
and queen, and her new friend Puck.

A *Midsummer Night's Dream* was first written hundreds of years ago by the most famous writer of all time, William Shakespeare. In his play, there are many other characters, including a rich duke and two young couples who fall in love, but the best-loved characters have always been the magical fairy folk and their king and queen, Oberon and Titania.

The fairies in the play have delightful names like Cobweb and Peaseblossom. And the magical flower "Love in Idleness" is a real plant—it's a small wild pansy.

The enchanting music was written by Felix Mendelssohn to go with the play. He started writing it when he was just 17 years old, and it is full of sparkling and scurrying sounds to help us imagine the silvery moonlight and fluttering fairy wings. You can even hear the sound of Bottom braying like a donkey!

The music for *A Midsummer Night's Dream* has been used for ballets many times. The adventures of the magical fairies in the moonlit forest is always lots of fun, and the scenery and costumes are wonderful to see.

If you could dress up as a magical elf or woodland fairy, what would your costume look like?